KATIE WOO and PEDRO Mysteries

The Mystery of the Box of Chocolates

by Fran Manushkin

illustrated by Tammie Lyon

PICTURE WINDOW BOOKS
a capstone imprint

Published by Picture Window Books, an imprint of Capstone
1710 Roe Crest Drive, North Mankato, Minnesota 56003
capstonepub.com

Text copyright © 2024 by Fran Manushkin
Illustrations copyright © 2024 by Capstone

All rights reserved. No part of this publication may be reproduced in whole or in part, or stored in a retrieval system, or transmitted in any form or by any means, electronic, mechanical, photocopying, recording, or otherwise, without written permission of the publisher.

Library of Congress Cataloging-in-Publication Data
Names: Manushkin, Fran, author. | Lyon, Tammie, illustrator. | Manushkin, Fran. Katie Woo and Pedro mysteries.
Title: The mystery of the box of chocolates / by Fran Manushkin ; illustrated by Tammie Lyon.
Description: North Mankato, Minnesota : Picture Window Books, an imprint of Capstone, [2024] | Series: Katie Woo and Pedro mysteries | Audience: Ages 5-7. | Audience: Grades K-1. | Summary: Katie has bought a box of chocolates for her mom's birthday, but when they go to open it the box is missing, and Katie and Pedro set out to track down the thief.
Identifiers: LCCN 2023020896 (print) | LCCN 2023020897 (ebook) | ISBN 9781484688618 (hardcover) | ISBN 9781484688625 (paperback) | ISBN 9781484688588 (pdf) | ISBN 9781484688670 (kindle edition) | ISBN 9781484688632 (epub)
Subjects: LCSH: Woo, Katie (Fictitious character)—Juvenile fiction. | Chinese Americans—Juvenile fiction. | Hispanic Americans—Juvenile fiction. | Birthdays—Juvenile fiction. | Gifts—Juvenile fiction. | CYAC: Chinese Americans—Fiction. | Hispanic Americans—Fiction. | Birthdays—Fiction. | Gifts—Fiction. | Mystery and detective stories. | LCGFT: Detective and mystery fiction.
Classification: LCC PZ7.M3195 Mu 2024 (print) | LCC PZ7.M3195 (ebook) | DDC 813.54 [E]—dc23/eng/20230516
LC record available at https://lccn.loc.gov/2023020896
LC ebook record available at https://lccn.loc.gov/2023020897

Design Elements by Shutterstock: Darcraft, Magnia
Designed by Dina Her

Table of Contents

Chapter 1
A Birthday...5

Chapter 2
Missing Chocolate!................................11

Chapter 3
Case Closed 20

Chapter 1

A Birthday

Pedro and his family came over to Katie's house for lunch. It was Katie's mom's birthday. They brought her a bunch of flowers.

Katie told her mom, "Close your eyes. I have a birthday surprise for you."

Katie's mom smiled. "I love your surprises."

"Okay," said Katie, "now you can open your eyes."

"It's a box of chocolates!" said her mom. "I'm wild about chocolate with cherries inside!"

"We knew that," said Katie's dad.

Katie smiled. "And I know that you love pretty candy boxes and red ribbons."

"For sure!" said her mom. "This box is so pretty. I don't want to open it. I want to keep looking at it."

"*Arf! Arf!*"

Koko sniffed the box and tugged the ribbon.

"Let go!" said Katie. "You can't eat chocolate. Chocolate is bad for dogs."

Chapter 2
Missing Chocolate!

Soon it was time for lunch. Katie took little bites of her chicken sandwich. Pedro took big bites.

After lunch, Katie's mom said, "Now let's have some candy."

She reached for the pretty chocolate box. "It's gone!" she yelled. "My chocolate is gone!"

"Oh no!" Katie cried. "You have to be mean to steal someone's birthday chocolate!"

Pedro was furious! He said, "Let's jump on our bikes and catch the candy thief before he eats it all up!"

"The box had a long red ribbon on it," said Katie. "I see something long and red up ahead. Is it a ribbon?"

No! It was a leash on a dog.

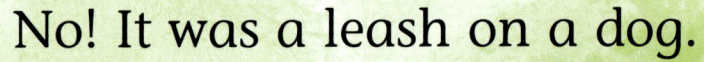

Katie pointed. "I see something skinny on that man's hot dog."

Was it a red ribbon from a present?

Of course not!

It was a long, tasty, hot pepper!

Then Katie saw someone she knew. It was her mail carrier.

"Hi!" said Katie. "Did you see someone with a pretty box?"

"Yes." The mail carrier pointed. "He went that way."

Chapter 3
Case Closed

Katie and Pedro started riding after the man!

"That man looks like my dad," said Katie. "Wait! It *is* my dad!"

Katie yelled, "Dad, what are you doing with Mom's candy? You are taking away her surprise."

"No," said her dad. "I am helping Mom get surprised! She always sneaks looks at her present. This time I am adding a surprise at the last minute."

Katie and her dad hurried home together. Katie helped her dad put the surprise in the box of candy.

When her mom opened the box, she was very happy.

Inside was a locket with a picture of Katie and her dad.

"Oh my!" said Katie's mom. "Your gift is as sweet as chocolate."

So were the hugs!

About the Author

Fran Manushkin is the author of Katie Woo, the highly acclaimed fan-favorite early-reader series, as well as the popular Pedro series. Her other books include *Happy in Our Skin*, *Plenty of Hugs!*, *Baby, Come Out!*, and the best-selling board books *Big Girl Panties* and *Big Boy Underpants*. There is a real Katie Woo: Fran's great-niece, but she doesn't get into as much trouble as the Katie in the books. Fran lives in New York City, three blocks from Central Park, where she can often be found bird-watching and daydreaming. She writes at her dining room table, without the help of her naughty cats, Goldy and Chaim.

About the Illustrator

Tammie Lyon, the illustrator of the Katie Woo and Pedro series, says that these characters are two of her favorites. Tammie has illustrated work for Disney, Scholastic, Simon and Schuster, Penguin, HarperCollins, and Amazon Publishing, to name a few. She is also an author/illustrator of her own stories. Her first picture book, *Olive and Snowflake*, was released to starred reviews from *Kirkus* and *School Library Journal*. Tammie lives in Cincinnati, Ohio, with her husband, Lee, and two dogs, Amos and Artie. She spends her days working in her home studio in the woods, surrounded by wildlife and, of course, two mostly-always-sleeping dogs.

Glossary

chocolate (CHAW-kuh-lit)—a sweet, brown food made from cocoa beans

furious (FYOOR-ee-uhs)—very angry

thief (THEEF)—someone who steals

locket (LOK-it)—a small case usually made out of metal that has a space for a photo and is often worn on a chain as a necklace

All About Mysteries

A mystery is a story where the main characters must figure out a puzzle or solve a crime. Let's think about *The Mystery of the Box of Chocolates.*

Plot

In a mystery, the plot focuses on solving a problem. What is the problem in this story?

Clues

To solve a mystery, readers often look for clues. Did Pedro and Katie have any clues in this mystery?

Red Herrings

Red herrings are bad clues. They do not help solve the mystery. Sometimes they even make the mystery harder to solve. Were there any red herrings in this story? Explain your answer.

Thinking About the Story

1. When the box of chocolates went missing, Katie's mom, Katie, and Pedro each had different reactions. How did each one react?

2. Katie kept thinking they saw a red ribbon as they looked for the missing box of chocolates. What were they actually seeing? Can you think of other things that are long, skinny, and red?

3. Write about a time something of yours was missing. How did you feel?

4. Pretend you are Katie's mom and write thank you notes for your birthday.

Cherry Chocolate Fudge

Katie's mom loves chocolates with cherries inside them. Here is an easy recipe that combines chocolate and cherries for a tasty homemade candy. Ask a grown-up to help you make a batch, and be sure to share your sweet treats with others!

What you need:

Ingredients

- 12 ounces of semi-sweet chocolate chips
- 16-ounce can of cherry frosting
- 16-ounce jar of maraschino cherries

Equipment

- 8 x 8-inch pan
- foil
- cooking spray
- glass bowl

What you do:

1. Line the pan with a piece of foil. Spray it with the cooking spray.

2. Drain your cherries, and dry them on a paper towel. Cut each cherry into four pieces.

3. Pour the chocolate chips into the glass bowl, and microwave them for 20 seconds. Stir. Repeat 1-2 times, or until completely melted and smooth.

4. Add the frosting and chopped cherries, and mix well. Pour into the prepared pan and smooth.

5. Refrigerate for one hour, and then cut into squares. Enjoy!

Solve more mysteries with Katie and Pedro!

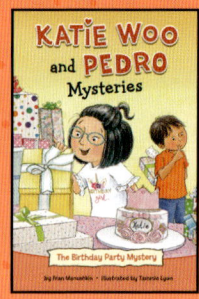 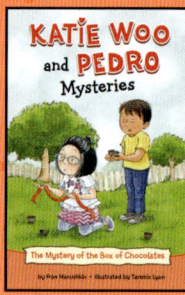 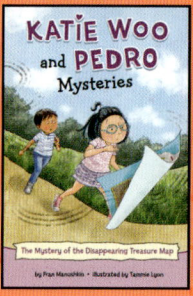 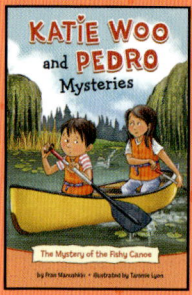
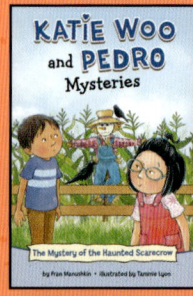 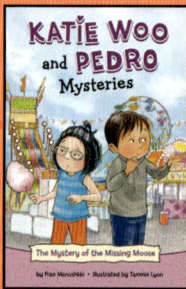 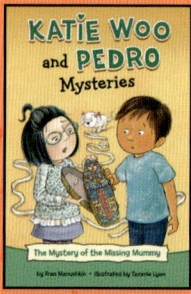 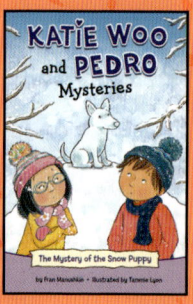
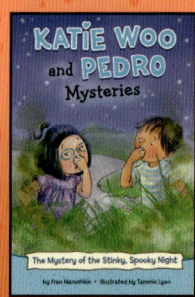 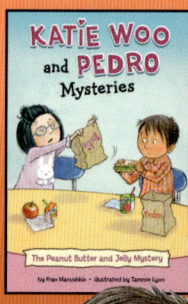 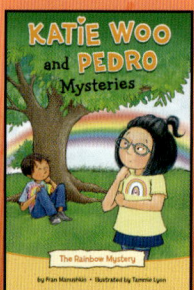 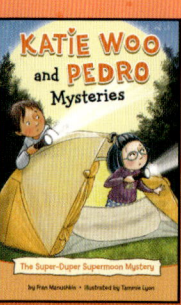